Up Went the Balloon

by Jenny Jinks and Maxine Lee

W

Dev had a balloon.

3

Up went the balloon.

It flew past a house.

Up went the balloon.

It flew past a nest.

Up went the balloon.

It flew past a tree.

Up went the balloon.

It flew past a bird.

Up went the balloon.

It flew past a cloud.

Up went the balloon.

It flew past a plane.

15

Up went the balloon.

It flew past a rocket.

The moon had a balloon!

Story trail

Start

Start at the beginning of the story trail. Ask your child to retell the story in their own words, pointing to each picture in turn to recall the sequence of events.

Independent Reading

This series is designed to provide an opportunity for your child to read on their own. These notes are written for you to help your child choose a book and to read it independently.

In school, your child's teacher will often be using reading books which have been banded to support the process of learning to read. Use the book band colour your child is reading in school to help you make a good choice. *Up Went the Balloon* is a good choice for children reading at Red Band in their classroom to read independently.

The aim of independent reading is to read this book with ease, so that your child enjoys the story and relates it to their own experiences.

About the book

Dev loves his balloon but a gust of wind blows it out of his hand. The balloon goes on an incredible journey up through the sky until finally stopping on the moon.

Before reading

Help your child to learn how to make good choices by asking: "Why did you choose this book? Why do you think you will enjoy it?" Support your child to think about what they already know about the story context. Look at the cover together and ask: "What do you think the story will be about?" Read the title aloud and ask: "What do you think happens to the balloon?"

Remind your child that they can try to sound out the letters to make a word if they get stuck.

Decide together whether your child will read the story independently or read it aloud to you. When books are short, as at Red Band, your child may wish to do both!

During reading

reading aloud, support your child if they hesitate or ask for help by
telling the word. Remind your child of what they know and what they
can do independently.

reading to themselves, remind your child that they can come and
ask for your help if stuck.

After reading

Support comprehension by asking your child to tell you about the
story. Use the story trail to encourage your child to retell the story
in the right sequence, in their own words.

Give your child a chance to respond to the story: "Did you have a
favourite part? Have you had a balloon before? Describe it."

Help your child think about the messages in the book that go beyond
the story and ask: "Why did the balloon keep going higher?" "Where
else could it have landed?"

Extending learning

Help your child extend the story structure by using the same
sentence pattern and adding some more elements. For example,
family are on a boat, and a child drops a stone overboard. "Down
sank the stone. It went past a fish."

On a few of the pages, check your child can finger point accurately
by asking them to show you how they kept their place in the print by
tracking from word to word.

Help your child to use letter information by asking them to find the
interest word on each page by using the first letter. For example:
"Which word is 'rocket'? How did you know it was that word?"

Franklin Watts
First published in Great Britain in 2019
by The Watts Publishing Group

Copyright © The Watts Publishing Group 2019

Series Editors: Jackie Hamley and Melanie Palmer
Series Advisors: Dr Sue Bodman and Glen Franklin
Series Designer: Peter Scoulding

A CIP catalogue record for this book is
available from the British Library.

ISBN 978 1 4451 6774 9 (hbk)
ISBN 978 1 4451 6776 3 (pbk)
ISBN 978 1 4451 6775 6 (library ebook)

Printed in China

Franklin Watts
An imprint of
Hachette Children's Group
Part of The Watts Publishing Group
Carmelite House
50 Victoria Embankment
London EC4Y 0DZ

An Hachette UK Company
www.hachette.co.uk

www.franklinwatts.co.uk

FSC
www.fsc.org
MIX
Paper from
responsible sources
FSC® C104740